For Birdie,
and all the other raptors
I've known

First edition 2014

Library of Congress Catalog Card Number 2013944012
ISBN 978-0-7636-6012-3

14 15 16 17 18 19 TLF 10 9 8 7 6 5 4 3 2 1

Printed in Dongguan, Guangdong, China

This book was typeset in Aunt Mildred.
The illustrations were done in pencil and watercolor, with some digital tweakery.

Candlewick Press
99 Dover Street
Somerville, Massachusetts 02144

visit us at www.candlewick.com

IF I HAD A RAPTOR

George O'Connor

CANDLEWICK PRESS

If I had a raptor,
I'd want to get her as a baby,
when she's all teensy and tiny
and funny and fluffy.

A baby raptor is so teensy and tiny

that she would be easy to lose.

I'd give her a little bell

so I could always find her.

Ring-a-ding-ding!

There you are!

Baby raptors are the cutest!

If I had a raptor,
she would like to sit on my lap,
and I would let her.

Even when she grows up,
she will still like to sit on my lap.

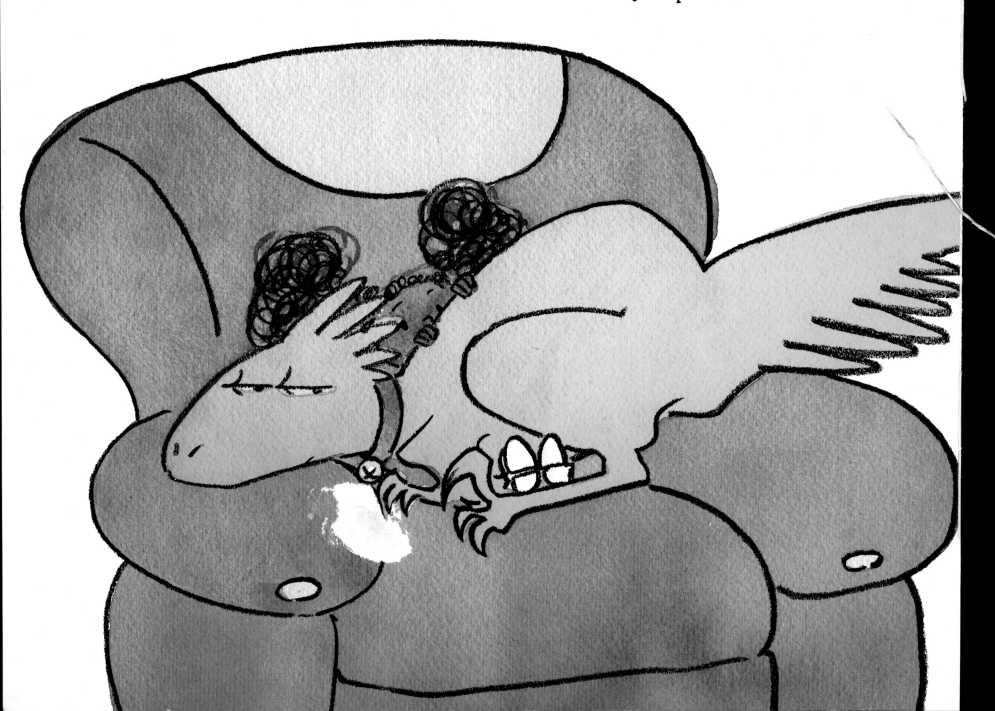

A raptor likes nothing better
than a nice warm spot.
My raptor would bask on
a sunny windowsill

or snuggle in the
clean laundry.

She would even settle on my homework.
Or in any cozy little space, really.

My raptor would like to sleep.

She would sleep a LOT.

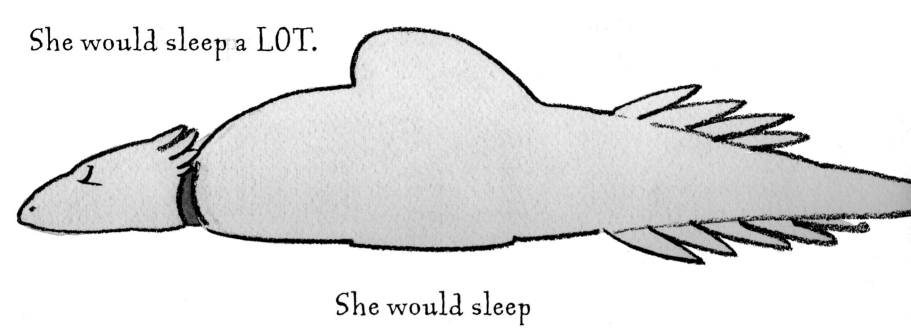

She would sleep

all

day

long.

Because she will probably
definitely run around like crazy.

She will run around like crazy
all
night
long.

Raptors have special eyes
that let them see in the dark.

No matter how late she stays up,
my raptor would wake me up nice and early.

She would let me know when she's hungry.

Or not.

If I had a raptor,
I would have to
teach her what's right
and what's wrong.

I might even have to
trim her claws a little bit
now and then.

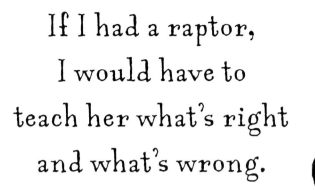

She would always
forgive me, though.

Good girl!

All raptors like to hunt.
If I had a raptor,
she would stalk the little things
that catch her eye, like birds,
or bugs, or even a dust bunny.

Sometimes she would
stare at nothing at all or
at I wouldn't even know what.

And sometimes
she might just stare at me.

If I had a raptor . . .

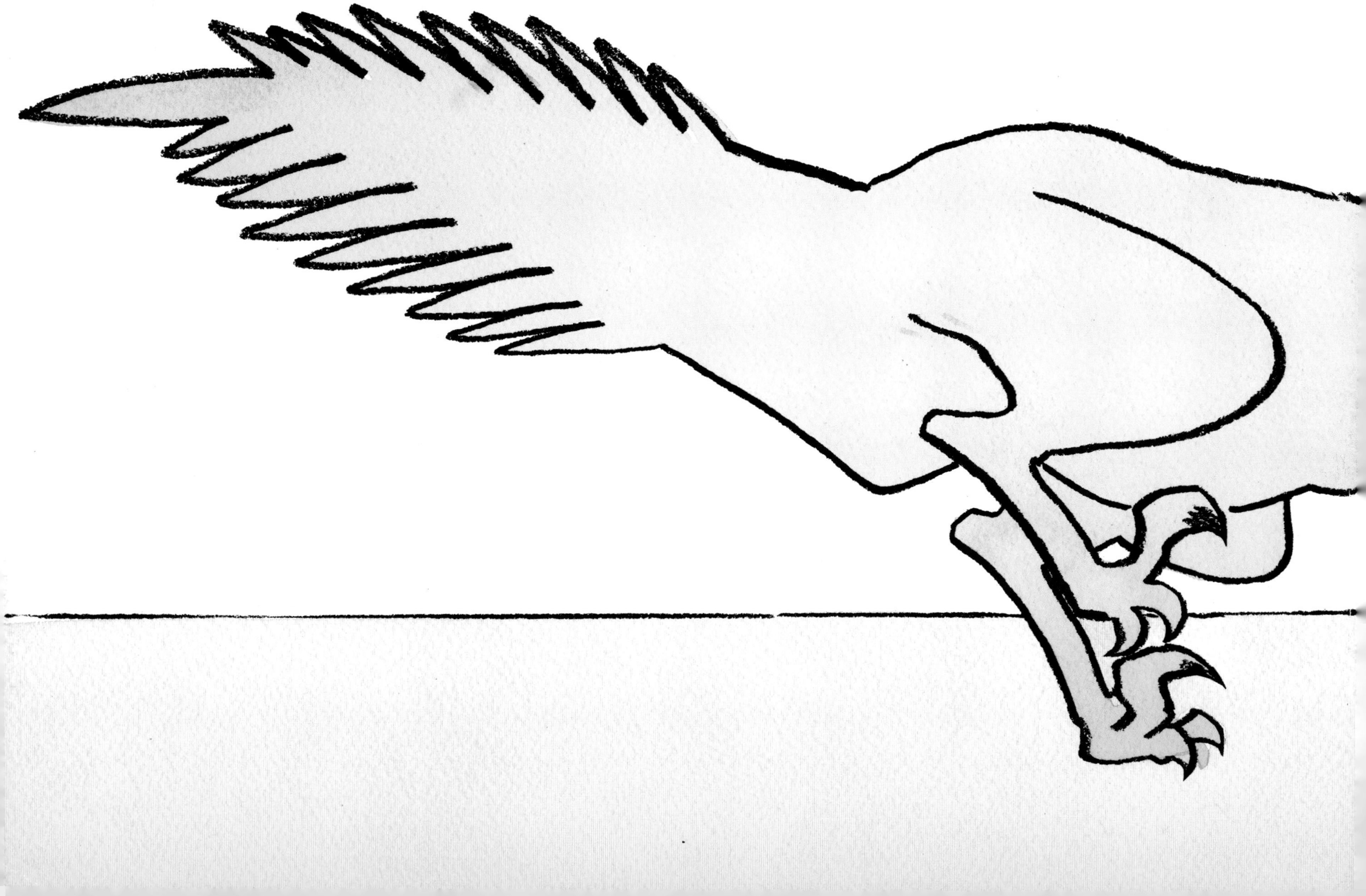

Ring-a-ding-ding!

There you are!

it would be the best thing ever.